IF HE HAD NOT COME

Original Story by
Nan F. Weeks

Reintroduced to a New Generation of Readers by
David Nicholson

Illustrated by Charlie Jaskiewicz

Going Deeper end notes by Josh Mulvihill

WestBow Press books may be ordered through booksellers or by contacting:

WestBow Press
A Division of Thomas Nelson & Zondervan
1663 Liberty Drive
Bloomington, IN 47403
www.westbowpress.com
1 (866) 928-1240

All proceeds of the sale of IF HE HAD NOT COME will be donated to the National Christian Foundation.

ISBN: 978-1-4908-1810-8 (hc)
ISBN: 978-1-4908-1811-5 (e)

Library of Congress Control Number: 2013921689

Printed in the United States of America.

WestBow Press rev. date: 5/22/2014

Printed in Canada by Friesens
Altona, Manitoba
June 2014
202850

WESTBOW®
PRESS
A DIVISION OF THOMAS NELSON
& ZONDERVAN

This book is dedicated

to my wife,

Barbara,

and our children and grandchildren.

May they continue the tradition

of sharing this wonderful story with

their own children and grandchildren.

PREFACE

While sitting in my adult Sunday School class, I heard Nan Weeks' story *If He Had Not Come* for the first time; and I must say, the story captivated me right from the start. I can remember driving home with my young family that very Sunday morning thinking to myself, "I am going to read this story to my family this and every Christmas to come."

It's been nearly thirty years, and the tradition of sharing this simple, thought-provoking story continues on.

And now, I would like to share it with you . . .

IT WAS CHRISTMAS EVE, and after Bobby carefully hung his stocking above the fireplace, he climbed the stairs to his room. Most of the time Bobby didn't like going to bed, but tonight he wanted to get to sleep so he'd be up bright and early on Christmas morning. He was looking forward to finding out what was in those packages under the Christmas tree!

Before he had gone up to his room, though, Bobby and his dad sat by the Christmas tree for their daily Bible reading. Some of Jesus' words to His friends in John 15:22 stayed with Bobby and kept circling through his mind even after he had climbed into bed. He whispered them over and over until he fell asleep. The five words were, "If I had not come."

It seemed like Bobby had hardly gone to sleep when a loud voice called, "Get up, Bobby, get up right away!" He sat up and rubbed his eyes. Was it morning? Was his dad calling to him already? He jumped out of bed and pulled on his clothes. He sure wondered if he was going to get the presents he wanted—new skates, a flashlight, a baseball, maybe that model airplane he'd seen at Woolworths! He hurried downstairs.

But all was still, and no lights were on. His dad wasn't waiting for him at the bottom of the stairs, his mother wasn't in the kitchen making breakfast. And the Christmas tree was gone! No stocking hanging above the fireplace, no wreaths in the window, *and no presents!*

Bobby ran over to the front door and looked up and down the street. He could hear the rumble of machinery from the large factory three blocks away. He grabbed his jacket and cap and raced to the factory entrance, but it was blocked by a grim-looking man. "What do you want, kid?" he growled.

"Why is the factory open on Christmas?" Bobby wanted to know.

"Christmas?" the man asked. "What's that? I've never heard of it. We're very busy right now, kid, so you clear out, you hear me?" Bobby frowned and turned away, puzzled and even a little scared. *What's going on?* he wondered as he started toward town.

Bobby hurried along the sidewalk. *Maybe I'll find someone else I can ask,* he thought. To his amazement, the stores were all open—on Christmas Day! The grocer, the barber, the baker—each of them busy with customers, and they impatiently replied to his question, "Christmas? What's that?" Bobby tried to explain it was Jesus' birthday, that the first part of the word *Christmas* means Jesus, but he was gruffly ordered to move on.

"Can't you see I'm busy?" the five-and-dime store owner demanded as Bobby turned away.

Walking slowly around the corner, Bobby suddenly thought, *I'll go to our church. There's going to be a special Christmas service this morning, and people will be there getting ready for it!* He ran the two blocks, but stopped short in front of a large vacant lot. "I guess I'm lost," he mumbled to himself. He looked around but soon decided this *had* to be the place. Then he noticed a large sign, and he read the words out loud: "IF I HAD NOT COME." *The same words Dad and I read last night,* he thought, amazed. *If Jesus hadn't come, there would be no church, no Christmas, no Christmas carols....*

He wandered away feeling sad and uncertain. *What can I do to celebrate Jesus' birth,* he wondered, *even if nobody else seems to know about it?* Then he remembered that his class had gathered up a box of toys and games to send to the Children's Home so the youngsters without families would have presents on Christmas morning. "I'll go there and watch them open their presents," he said out loud, already feeling better. But when he found the street where the home for kids was supposed to be, only the gate was left. And instead of seeing "Children's Home" on the archway, he read, "IF I HAD NOT COME."

He turned away, disappointed and sad once more. He came upon an old man, looking frail and ill, and Bobby said, "Hello, Mister. I guess you're sick. Let's go to the hospital up the road." The man put his hand on Bobby's shoulder, and they started out. But the poor man couldn't walk very fast, so Bobby said he would run on ahead and tell them to send an ambulance. "They'll get you well again," Bobby said. "You wait. Here, I'll help you sit down on this bench till we're back."

IF I HAD
NOT COME
I HAD NOT COM
IF I HAD NOT COME
IF
I HAD
NOT
COME
IF I HAD
NOT
COME
IF I HAD
NOT COME
IF I HAD
NOT
COME
IF I
NOT
OME

Bobby ran back towards town and the fine hospital. He knew right where it would be, too, on the corner.... But he stopped short when he saw only a busy intersection filled with signs and posters and the words on each one, "IF I HAD NOT COME." What could he do? The old man needed help! *Oh, yes, the homeless shelter...they'll know how to help my friend.* He hurried on his way.

Bobby remembered that the shelter was just down the street from where the hospital used to be, and he was sure the kind people there would take in his new friend who needed care. But when he came to the building, instead of a warm welcome and people ready to help, he saw angry faces and a group of men gambling. They swore at him when he asked if they could help his friend. Then he noticed over the door the same words, "IF I HAD NOT COME." Bobby sighed. He sure didn't know where else to turn. Then all at once he knew what to do. "Oh," he exclaimed out loud. "I'll go home! Dad and Mother will know what to do for my sick friend!"

He ran all the way home, scrambled up the steps, and in the front door. On the way through the living room, he stopped to pick up the Bible his father had read from the night before. Puffing from his run, he began turning quickly past the pages of the Old Testament to find the Gospel of John and those words, "If I had not come." But when he thumbed beyond the book of Malachi, the last one of the Old Testament, *the rest of the pages were blank!* All he could see was a faint outline on each, "IF I HAD NOT COME." Bobby sat down, stunned at the thought of a world without Jesus. "No Christmas, no churches," he whispered, "no places to help people who are sick, homeless, or in need..."

And then he heard the sound of bells.... "The chimes from church," Bobby exclaimed, jumping out of bed. He looked around. "Hey, I'm in my own room! And they're playing my favorite Christmas carol, 'Joy to the World, the Lord is Come'!" Then he heard his mother's voice from the bottom of the stairs, "Merry Christmas, Bobby! I thought you were going to get up early this morning."

Bobby couldn't help laughing, so glad it was just a bad dream. "But maybe more than a dream," he said to himself. He knelt by his bed and prayed, "Lord Jesus, I'm so glad You *did* come. You are the very best Christmas present anyone can have. I'll show You my thanks by doing everything I can to please You today and every day. Help me to be the kind of boy You want me to be."

IF HE HAD NOT COME
Interactive Topics for Families and Sunday School Teachers

These are suggestions only, and the goal is not a "right" answer but open-ended questions that will encourage interaction and discussion. Invite other questions from the children about particular aspects of the characters and the story.

1. When Bobby went to bed on Christmas Eve, what do you think it was about the words in John 15:22, "If I had not come," that stayed with him until he fell asleep? Was he starting to imagine his world without Jesus? What would our life be like without Him?

2. What did Jesus mean when He said, "If I had not come and spoken to them, they would not have been guilty of sin, but now they have no excuse for their sin"? (John 15:22) What do you think sin is? Why did Jesus tell His listeners they would have no excuse for their sin?

3. When you hear someone calling for you to get up on Christmas morning, what's the first thing that comes to your mind? Is there anything wrong with imagining the gifts we might find under the tree? What other things would be good to think about on Christmas morning along with the presents?

4. Put yourself in Bobby's place as he walked into his living room...everything having anything to do with Christmas was completely gone! Would you wonder if a thief had broken in and stolen everything? Would you be frightened? How else would you feel?

5. Bobby went into town to find out what was going on, and to his amazement found all the stores were open. This was happening at a time when stores usually closed on Sundays, and certainly on Christmas Day, in honor of Jesus. What would you find open or closed on Christmas Day in your town? Why do you think stores close on Christmas these days? Is it to honor Jesus, or for some other reasons?

6. Bobby discovered it was an awful world without Christmas, or church, or hospitals, or places where needy people could get help. Imagine driving up to your church and seeing just an empty field of grass. What would you think? What are some other things that would be different if Jesus had not come to Earth? Make a list of ideas. Illustrate them, or act them out, or create your own written version of *If He Had Not Come.*

Going Deeper
by Josh Mulvihill

Few would argue that Jesus Christ has influenced the lives of more people than any other person in history. Emperors, governors, and presidents have come and gone, but it's Jesus and His birth that we still celebrate today, some two thousand years later! The impact of His life is everywhere: our laws, calendar, moral and cultural priorities, education, health care, and the arts. As a family or class, explore what the Bible says about the birth of Jesus by asking children the following questions:

1. **How do you think life would be different if Jesus had not come to Earth as a baby?** (If children have difficulty answering this question, consider these discussion starters.)
   * Today's calendar year would be different as it is based on the birth of Jesus.
   * Many of today's schools, universities and hospitals, including some in your area, would not be in existence nor would the local YMCA, Habitat for Humanity, and world-relief organizations like Salvation Army, World Vision, and Compassion International. The tragic result would be increased suffering, starvation, and neglected orphans worldwide.

2. **According to the Bible, why did Jesus come to Earth?** (The Bible clearly states why Jesus came to Earth. Read the following verses together, pointing out the many reasons why God sent Jesus to Earth.)
   * To deliver us from sin (John 1:29)
   * To destroy the power of death (Hebrews 2:14)
   * To defeat Satan (1 John 3:8 and 1 John 4:1—3)
   * To fulfill the law (Matthew 5:17—18)
   * To seek and save the lost (Luke 19:10)
   * To serve and to give His life as a ransom for many (Mark 10:45)
   * To reveal God the Father (Matthew 11:27)

3. **What would it mean for us spiritually if Jesus had not come to Earth?** (Read the Bible together as a family or class, pointing out the importance of Jesus coming to Earth as a baby.)
   * If Jesus had not come, we would only know God in part (Hebrews 1:1—2).
   * If Jesus had not come, we would not know the fullness of God's love (John 15:13).
   * If Jesus had not come, there would be no salvation for sinners (Romans 5:8, 10).

4. **For further study, read Matthew 1:19—25. According Matthew 1: 21, why did Jesus come to Earth?** (Jesus came to save His people from their sin. Sin is rebellion and wrongdoing. The penalty for sin is eternity in hell. Jesus came to pay for our sin and make us His children because of His great love for us. Invite children to respond to the gospel message.)

The Gospel Message

God is a gift-giving God! He wants to give good gifts to those He loves. Christmas is a time when we remember the best gift of all—salvation through Jesus Christ. This gift will not be found in a wrapped package sitting under the tree. The best gift came as a little baby, wrapped and laid in a manger. At Christmas we remember that Jesus lived a perfect life and died on a cross to pay for our sin (1 Peter 2:24). Receiving God's gift of salvation is as easy as A-B-C!

A – Admit you are a sinner separated from a perfect God

The Bible begins with bad news; we are sinners. Romans 3:23 states, "For all [including children] have sinned." Sin is rebellion (Isaiah 1:2), disobedience (Romans 5:19), and wrongdoing (1 John 5:17). We sin when we act as if we are the king of our life and live apart from God's rule. All who have sinned are guilty before God, dead in sin, and awaiting condemnation (Ephesians 2:1—3). The penalty for sin is death and hell. God is a loving God, but He is also a perfect God who does not ignore or excuse sin. God always deals with sin. That is bad news and a big problem for each of us.

B – Believe in your heart that Jesus is Savior

The Bible also has good news; Jesus died to pay for our sins! Ephesians 2:8 states, "For by grace you have been saved through faith. And this is not your own doing; it is the gift of God." There is nothing we can do to be saved from sin apart from believing in Jesus (John 14:6). To believe in Jesus is to fully trust that Jesus is Savior and fully rely on God for salvation. The Bible teaches us how to believe. It says, "Believe in your heart that God raised [Jesus] from the dead, [and] you will be saved" (Romans 10:9). When we believe God, we accept what He says as true and run to Him.

C – Confess with your mouth and receive God's gift of salvation

Gifts must be received and the gift of salvation is no different; we must repent and receive God's gift of salvation. To repent is to turn away from sin and be sorry for doing what is wrong (Acts 3:19). Romans 10:9 tells us, "Confess with your mouth that Jesus is Lord." To confess is to agree with God that Jesus is King and that we are sinful and need a Savior. When we do this, John 1:12 has great news, "But to all who did receive him, who believed in his name, he gave the right to become children of God." Those who place their trust in Jesus will no longer be guilty of wrongdoing, but will be in a right relationship with God.

Are you interested in receiving God's gift of salvation?

If you are interested in placing your trust in Jesus, then repeat the following prayer: *"Dear God, I believe Jesus is your Son. Thank you that Jesus died on the cross for the wrong things I have done. I understand that I have rebelled against You. Please forgive me for my sin. I invite Jesus to take my penalty and be the ruler of my life. Please help me to love and obey Jesus all my life. In Jesus name I pray, amen."*

An Idea to Help You Celebrate Christmas . . .

Draw a green Christmas tree complete with lights, a star on top, and gifts below; and as you draw, consider how a Christmas tree reminds us of eternal life in Jesus:

- Jesus died on a cross, made from a tree.
- A fresh pine tree is always green, signifying never-ending life in Jesus.
- A tree points to the heavens, reminding us to keep our eyes fixed on Jesus.
- The star on top represents the star that led the wise men to Jesus.
- Lights remind us of the glory of the Lord revealed through a host of angels that appeared to the shepherds.
- Gifts remind us of the four gifts (gold, frankincense, myrrh, and worship) the wise men gave to Jesus and the gift of salvation through Jesus Christ.

Soon to come
IF HE HAD NOT COME
Script for stage plays

For more information check out this website:
www.davids-treehouse.com

Nan F. Weeks was a teacher and a writer of stories and curriculum for children, and her original version of this story was included in an anthology, *Christ and the Fine Arts,* by Cynthia Maus, originally published in 1938. Anyone with further information about the author of the original narrative, please contact David Nicholson at www. davids-treehouse.com.

David Nicholson, a retired teacher, discovered Nan Weeks' story when his own children were young. He has taken on the rewarding mission of resurrecting and reintroducing it to a new generation of families, now with classic-style illustrations, suggested topics for discussion, and further information for "going deeper" into matters of the Christian faith. David and his wife, Barbara, currently reside in St. Paul, Minnesota. They have two married daughters and two grandchildren.

Charles Jaskiewicz has illustrated many religious and children's books. He currently lives in Warren, Ohio, with his wife, Judy. They have one daughter and three grandchildren. He may be contacted at craskiewicz@yahoo.com.

Josh Mulvihill is the pastor to children and families at Grace Church in Eden Prairie, Minnesota, and an adjunct professor at Crown College. He is completing his PhD at Southern Seminary. Josh is married to Jen and they have four children.

And a special thank you to

Gary and Carol Johnson, J&J Literary Advisors, brought their professional experience and expertise to the many details of getting this book ready for print.